Footlights and Fairy Dust

Matt and Maria go to the Theatre

Maren C. Tirabassi

Illustrated by Brandie Kramer

PublishingWorks
60 Winter Street
Exeter, New Hampshire 03833
(603) 778-9883
www.publishingworks.com

Design by Kathy Mack

LCCN: 2006903040
ISBN-13: 978-1-933002-26-2

Orders:
Revolution Booksellers
60 Winter Street
Exeter, New Hampshire
03833

800-REV-6603

Printed in China

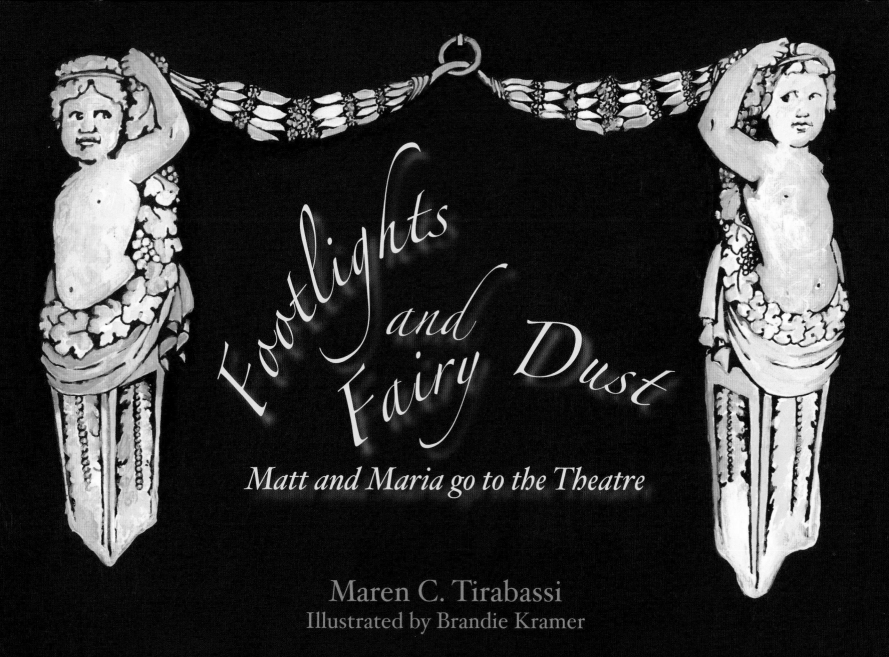

Footlights and Fairy Dust

Matt and Maria go to the Theatre

Maren C. Tirabassi
Illustrated by Brandie Kramer

PublishingWorks, Inc.
2007

All children love shows, but not all of them get the chance to explore a major theatre. Matt and Maria think they are the luckiest children in Boston, and they may be right. Their father is the manager of a wonderful old playhouse on Boylston Street called the Colonial Theatre. All sorts of great plays are staged at the Colonial, and they go to almost all of them. On stage right now is *Peter Pan*.

Matt and Maria's theatre was built inside a ten-story office building in 1900. It was designed by the architect Clarence Blackall on the site of the old Boston Public Library, opposite the Boston Common. In December, holiday lights sparkle on the trees in the Common. In the summer, tourists wander up and down, asking directions to the swan boats. In the fall and spring, college students and shoppers hurry to the subway. In all seasons, people stop under the **marquee** and read the theatre **houseboards**.

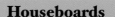

Marquee

A marquee is a lighted roof above the entrance to a theatre. Some marquees have built-in signs that announce the name of the show and its actors.

Houseboards

Houseboards are large posters on either side of the theatre's entrance which advertise the shows that are either playing or coming soon.

Matt and Maria usually attend a **matinee**, but sometimes they come to an evening performance. That's very exciting! However, if it's a school night, their mom and dad always insist that they go home before the show is over so they can get up for school the next day.

"Not fair!" they say. It's one of the few times Matt and Maria agree. Usually they fight more than Peter Pan and Captain Hook!

Tonight is Friday night, not a school night. Matt and Maria are coming to see *Peter Pan*. Maybe tonight they can stay through the end of the show.

Matinee
A matinee is a performance of a show that takes place in the afternoon.

Some weeks there is no show playing at the Colonial. Those are called "dark" weeks. Tonight the Colonial is "lit," and it's a magical place. Even the outer lobby is very elegant. Matt and Maria walk up to a box office window where a sign reads, "Today's Performance." A sign over the other window says, "Advance Sales."

"Picking up tickets for Matt and Maria," Matt says. He is in the fifth grade and is tall enough to see into the box office window. Mr. Moe or Miss Ina could buzz them in the pass door, but they like to come through the main entrance. Maria, who is in second grade, gets to hold the tickets. The inner lobby doors open at a half-hour before showtime. Maria hands their tickets to their friend Mr. Jimmy, the ticket taker. Mr. Jimmy and the ushers used to count torn tickets to see how many people were in the audience. Now the computer prints tickets and Mr. Jimmy scans them. Some people like to keep their tickets—"to paste in their diaries," Maria says. "I've been saving ticket stubs and playbills ever since I was a little girl."

Matt rolls his eyes. He thinks she is still pretty "little."

Matt and Maria's tickets say "comp," which means "complimentary." Maria thinks that means she is beautiful. Matt makes a choked noise in his throat. "No way," he says. "It just means 'free.' " Matt is, after all, the big brother—two years bigger.

"Three school years," Matt says.

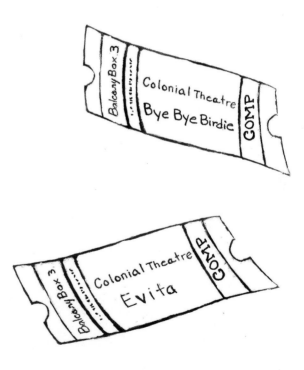

3

After their tickets are torn, they go into the inner lobby. It is beautiful, too—a hall of mirrors made to imitate Versailles Palace near Paris, France. Maria feels like a princess . . . but she doesn't think Matt feels like a prince.

Matt and Maria want to be shown to their seats by Miss Alice, even though they know the location of every numbered seat in the **house**.

Miss Alice is the chief usher—the very best of all the ushers—and the ushers at the Colonial are the best ushers in Boston, and the Boston ushers are the best theatre ushers in the whole world. They wear black dresses with white collars. Miss Alice gets to wear a beautiful black cloak to keep her warm on chilly nights.

Sometimes people try to seat themselves and they get all mixed up. Sometimes two people claim to have the same seat! Then the usher shines a flashlight on the tickets and points them toward the correct aisle. The ushers are very nice about helping patrons find their seats.

But the ushers are very fierce when people take pictures, especially after the announcement

that no photography is allowed because it endangers the actors.

Matt says that the people who have their cameras confiscated are often the same people who elbow children (even princesses) out of the way at the concession stand in the lobby. These theatre patrons aren't hungrier than everyone else. They just don't think the rules apply to them. Matt doesn't like it when grown-ups push his little sister around. That's his job.

Maria likes to buy Junior Mints from the concession stand, even though her father thinks that because they just had supper at the restaurant on the corner, they don't need anything more to eat. This restaurant is known for its very good ice cream. The children and their father always order ice cream.

"That was then, and now is now," Maria explains.

House
The house is the auditorium where the audience sits to watch a show. The downstairs seats are called the orchestra (this is not the same thing as the orchestra pit, where the musicians sit). One floor up is the mezzanine. Some of the best seats are here, because audience members can look down at the stage. Two floors up is the balcony. These seats are very high up, almost to the ceiling.

There is another group of people who are not Matt and Maria's favorites. They come late, after the house lights are down. They come even after the overture—which is music just for latecomers. They always seem to have seats in the center of a row down front. "Excuse me, excuse me," they say. It's very disturbing to the rest of the audience.

Matt and Maria love it when the latecomers have to wait in the lobby and miss the first part of the show. Their father agrees. Their mother says that is not a very charitable attitude.

Tonight Matt and Maria don't have to worry about latecomers walking in front of them because their "comp" seats are in the boxes. The boxes are on the side of the house. Very fashionable people used to sit in the boxes so that their friends could see their clothes. But now the boxes are often unsold because the view of the stage is not as clear there as the view from the orchestra.

Matt and Maria love the box seats because it's like having their own private room.

There are many different types of shows at the Colonial, but all of them are wonderful!

Matt and Maria like to list their favorite shows.

There are shows with music—called musicals—like *Big River*, which is about Huckleberry Finn. That was Maria's first full show. Other shows are plays, like *Dracula*. Matt calls that his first show, even though he was really just a baby. Matt loves *Dracula* because it's scary! The actor who played Dracula let their father try on his cape. It was heavy, even for a grown-up!

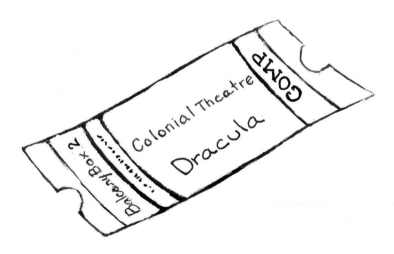

Another scary show Matt has seen is *The Phantom of the Opera*. Maria didn't "see" it, since she was hiding her head in her daddy's lap.

"I saw *Little Shop of Horrors*," Maria adds.

"That's not scary!" says Matt. "Man-eating plants are funny!"

"Let's list the happy shows," she says.

"Those are the ones that get good **reviews**."

Theatre Reviews

Reviews are descriptions of a show written by theatre critics that appear online or in a newspaper, on television, or on the radio. Critics give their opinions about the show—Is the show good, or not? People often decide whether or not to buy tickets to a show because of reading or hearing a review.

It's intermission!

One of the best things about a show is the intermission. Matt and Maria get to go through the pass door to the inner office to eat (more) candy. Everyone watches them as they go into this special place, and know that they are theatre kids. They are not as special as the acting children who play Wendy, Michael, and John, but they don't have to stand around the lobby listening to their parents like all the other children.

They listen to special people. During intermission the **Company Manager**, the **Press Agent**, the box office staff, the House Manager (that's Dad), and even the producer are all in the inner office. They are usually talking about exciting things—like how many tickets were sold, where the New York opening-night party will be, and how exciting it is to see Cathy Rigby—who is playing Peter Pan—fly.

But everybody stops to ask Matt and Maria how they like the show.

They love *Peter Pan*. They would give it the best review in the world!

"If kids don't like the theatre, then it will die," Matt says later.

He sounds a little pompous. Fifth graders are like that. Still, he is only repeating what other people have said . . . many, many times.

Company Manager

The Company Manager takes care of all the business matters for the show, including paying the cast and crew, making travel arrangements, and finding hotels or apartments for everyone in each city. The show gets paid by the number of tickets sold at the box office. The Company Manager is very happy when every ticket is sold!

Press Agent

The Press Agent arranges publicity for the newspapers, television, radio, and the Internet so that people in each city will know about the show and want to come to the theatre and see it.

One of the worst things about a show is the intermission!

Tonight Matt and Maria's father leaves his assistant in charge so he can take them home.

"But we want to see it to the end."

"You saw it to the end last Sunday afternoon!"

"Yes," said Matt, "but it might be different. Maybe this time the crocodile will eat him."

"We want to see the curtain calls and the flowers for the leading lady . . ."

"You mean leading boy," says Matt.

Someday Maria would like to hand out the flowers.

Someday Maria would like to be a leading lady . . . or Peter Pan. But only acting—because, unlike Peter Pan, she wants to grow up! Then she will always be able to stay till the end of the show!

"Tomorrow you can come and watch the matinee—again. Now we have to take the subway home. Do you want to come tomorrow?"

"Yes!" says Matt. "Yes!" Maria yells. Then she realizes that there are other people in the office. "Yes, thank you, Dad," she says. She is, after all, a princess.

Flash! Flash! go the lobby lights to remind all the people to finish their candy and drinks and find their seats. When the audience goes back into the house after the intermission, Matt and Maria put on their coats to go home. Some of the theatre employees, like the box office staff and most of the ushers, go home. Sometimes people leave who don't like the show. Sometimes even theatre critics leave to file their reviews for newspaper or television deadlines.

"How can they tell if a show is good or bad without seeing the end?" Maria asks.

Nobody can answer her.

The next day is Saturday. Matt and Maria come to the theatre at noon. They love the theatre in the daytime on Saturdays, as well as on snow days and during school vacations. This is because Matt and Maria have the theatre to themselves in the hours before the cast, **crew**, and audience arrive.

This is what they do when they come to the theatre in the daytime: First, they climb the iron spiral staircase from the box office to their father's office. ("Hello, Mr. Moe. Hello, Miss Ina.") Several times.

Their mother slipped and fell down the spiral stairs eleven days before Matt was born.

Maria says that explains a lot!

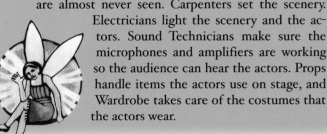

Crew

The Crew makes everything work backstage, and they are almost never seen. Carpenters set the scenery. Electricians light the scenery and the actors. Sound Technicians make sure the microphones and amplifiers are working so the audience can hear the actors. Props handle items the actors use on stage, and Wardrobe takes care of the costumes that the actors wear.

Matt and Maria fool around in the office while their dad makes phone calls. They draw pictures, play cards, and photocopy their own hands. Their dad has a telephone receptionist named Mrs. Philomena who answers the phone in the afternoon. When people ask her if their ticket locations are good, she says in a very frosty voice, "All the seats face the stage!"

Soon they are very bored. They go downstairs. "Hello, Mr. Moe. Hello, Miss Ina." They count the pictures of the many shows that have played the theatre. Maria's favorite is a photograph of the cast of *Annie*.

Annie played the Colonial for a long **run**.

Run
A run is the number of weeks a show plays at a theatre. Shows usually play eight times a week, including two or three matinees. The rest are evening performances.

In the picture of the *Annie* cast, there are lots of little girls. Each one had a mother who came with her. Stage mothers can be very demanding, and it made Matt and Maria's father's life difficult. (He calls it "more complicated.")

The great British actor Sir Laurence Olivier played the tragic hero in *Becket* at Matt and Maria's theatre before they were born. Becket was stabbed many times with swords. (Matt likes this part of the story.) Almost twenty years later Sir Laurence brought his own children to see *Annie*. The mothers told Ms. Nance, the press agent, to bring Sir Laurence eight programs and ask him to autograph them for their little girls. Sir Laurence not only did it—he also walked over from the Ritz-Carlton Hotel across the Public Garden and Boston Common to deliver them personally.

Both Matt and Maria wish they had been there that day!

After a while Matt and Maria become bored even with counting the pictures, so they go into the ladies' lounge, where Matt likes to roll his matchbox cars on the big onyx table. Maria says Matt shouldn't go in there because it is only for ladies. Matt says that's silly—the ladies' lounge is one of the most important places in the theatre's history. Many significant things happened there. In 1943 Richard Rodgers and Oscar Hammerstein rewrote the songs and story for *Oklahoma!* (which was originally called *Away We Go!* when it tried out in Boston) on that very table. It became one of the greatest shows of the century.

The onyx table is great for racing matchbox cars. Matt does not think it's such a good place for Maria to sprawl on when she looks at the ceiling painted with clouds and cherubs, surrounded by flowers and gold leaf (she calls them "gold leaves"). H. P. Pennell was the artist. When it comes to decor, Matt prefers the gentlemen's room, which is in the basement. It is a plain room with brown wood paneling, but nothing very famous ever happened there.

Maria likes to play hide-and-seek in the ladies' lounge. There is a couch behind a screen in the corner for ladies who have "the vapors" during a show. Matt says that means they ate too much candy and feel sick. There is a special entrance to the coatroom and the place where they keep the big ice machine. And, of course, there is the room just for women which has the toilets. Matt doesn't go in there, even when the theatre is empty!

Most exciting of all, the whole back wall of the ladies' lounge is a secret door. If you push on it in just the right way, you can escape and go into the office building's lobby. When they first discovered this magic door, they thought it was a dream come true. However, an office building is not nearly as interesting as the theatre, so they don't go exploring there anymore.

Still, they are ready. If there is ever a fire alarm in the Colonial, they can lead the rest of the audience safely out to the street.

If Matt and Maria's father has really long telephone calls, he forgets that they are there. Matt and Maria go on into the house. In the daytime, unless there is a rehearsal, there are no actors, no musicians, no stagehands. There is only one light on the stage. It is called a ghost light, and it has a single bulb on a tall metal stand.

That single lightbulb in the middle of the stage shines on the set. There are many shadows, and it's spooky. Matt tells Maria that this is when the ghosts of actors and actresses who have played in the theatre come out to haunt it.

"Oooooo," she says. This is very exciting as long as she is close to her big brother.

Matt tells her about some of the ghosts. Ethel Barrymore is here. She played in *Captain Jinks of the Horse Marines*. Every man in Boston fell in love with her because she was so pretty. She is the great-aunt of Drew Barrymore, who acts in movies today.

Maude Adams is here. She was the first person to play *Peter Pan* in America. When she was going to school, Matt and Maria's great-grandmother saw Maude Adams in *Peter Pan*, the first week it played in Boston in 1906.

"I bet she didn't have to go home at intermission!" Maria said.

Maude Adams as Peter Pan.

There are more ghosts. The Marx Brothers played here—they are very funny ghosts. There are Fred and Adele Astaire, who are dancing ghosts, and also brother and sister, just like Matt and Maria. And there are acting ghosts—Helen Hayes, Vincent Price, Paul Robeson, Richard Burton, Katharine Hepburn . . .

"Stop!" yells Maria. "Too many ghosts!"

"And there's Gus . . ."

Maria knows that Gus, the theatre cat in *Cats*, boasts about raising ghosts in an empty theatre.

"But *Cats* didn't play here!"

Cats didn't play at the Colonial—it played at the Shubert Theatre around the corner. So if there is any feline haunting, it would be around the corner, too.

"Oh yeah," Matt agrees. "You're right."

Big brothers don't know everything!

Dancing Ghosts
Fred and Adele
Astaire

"Now!" Matt says. This is their favorite part of a day at the theatre. Sometimes their father has been working so long on booking and advertising, getting the payroll together, and getting the cleaning company to come in and take care of bubblegum on an orchestra seat, he forgets that Matt and Maria are even there. Then they can play the never-go-there's.

Father says, "Never go in the orchestra pit."

Matt and Maria go in the orchestra pit. This is where the musicians sit to play for the show. It is sunk below stage level and only the conductor can see the actors. The musicians work hard, but sometimes, they look bored. Some even read a book or a magazine during a show!

Some shows, like *Chicago* and *Cabaret*, have the musicians right on stage. Then they need to look interested.

Of course, both *Cabaret* and *Chicago* are shows Matt and Maria have not been allowed to see . . . like *Sweeney Todd, the Demon Barber of Fleet Street*.

"We miss the best shows," Matt complains.

There are many places to hide in the theatre. Matt knows most of them. Someday he's going to hide and see a forbidden show. Maybe he could hide in the **scene dock**.

Maria would like a "sleepover" in the Colonial some night. She would bring her girlfriends. She doesn't care about forbidden shows . . . yet.

Scene Dock
The scene dock is a storage area for scenery which is located off stage. It is usually very full.

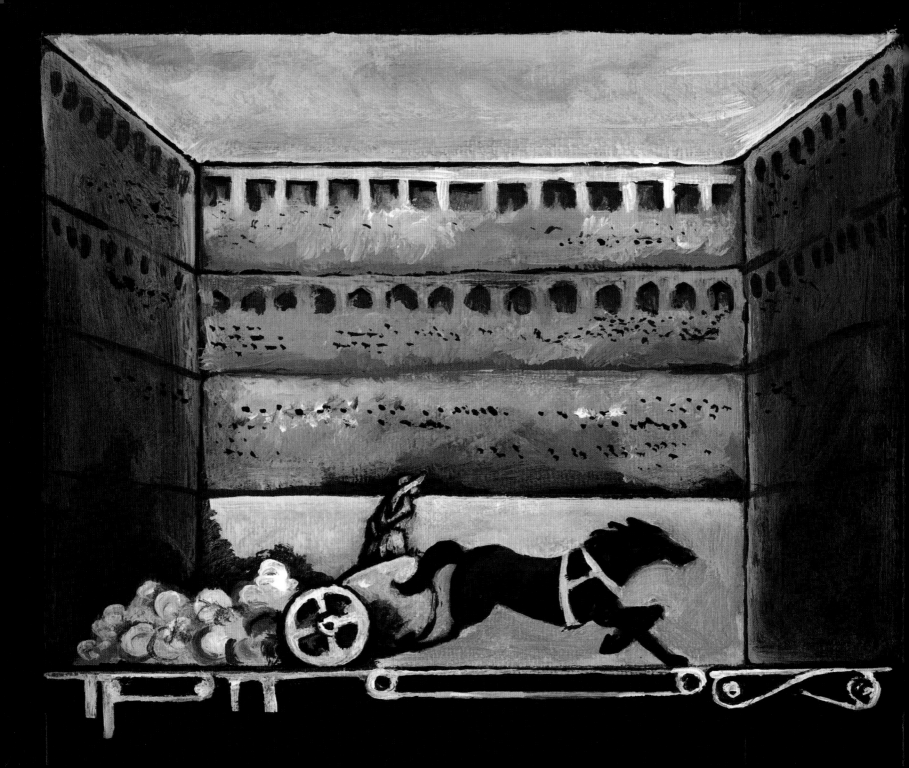

Father says, "Never go under the stage."

Matt and Maria go under the stage. This is where the **trapdoors** are. The very first show ever to play in the theatre was called *Ben-Hur*. That was in 1900, and it had a real Roman chariot race with real horses and chariots. It took four treadmills for the horses. There was also a shipwreck. That is why they need trapdoors on two hidden floors.

"Never go in the dressing rooms."

This is where the actors change out of their street clothes and put on their costumes and stage makeup. There are two big dressing rooms downstairs which are shared by all the members of the chorus.

There are two dressing rooms on the stage level for stars, like Julie Harris, James Earl Jones, Tommy Tune, or, of course, Cathy Rigby. There are thirty-five little dressing rooms upstairs for the in-between actors. These days most shows don't have thirty five in-between actors.

When the **Assistant Stage Manager** says, "Half-hour! Half-hour, please!" everyone is sitting at their dressing tables with very bright lights and big mirrors. They put on makeup. Some actors wear wigs or false beards. They become pirates and lost boys, Tiger Lily's band, and even Nana the dog. One actor puts on a hook.

Trapdoors
Trapdoors open into one or two basements from the stage. They provide space for sunken stairways and disappearing scenery, and a way for actors to descend or rise mysteriously.

Assistant Stage Manager
The Assistant Stage Manager handles all backstage details and emergencies, and is particularly responsible for seeing that the actors are ready to go on stage at the right time.

"Never ever go in the dressing rooms."

The dressing rooms are locked in the daytime. Even though they know this, Matt and Maria try to go in. They would like to try on some of the costumes, and they are sure they could put them back so nobody could tell, but wardrobe masters and mistresses are very fierce. They can be even fiercer than ushers. So it's probably a good thing the rooms are locked.

Instead, the children go into the **prop** man's office. Prop people are not so fierce. In fact, they are very nice and have lots of things that kids can touch—like swords and paintbrushes!

Props
Props (or Properties) include stage furniture, decorations (like rugs or flowers), and hand-held articles that the actors use in a show

Wings
The Wings are the offstage areas located immediately on the right and the left of the stage.

Stage Manager
The Stage Manager is responsible for the smooth running of a show from the first rehearsal to the last performance. The Stage Manager also calls all the light, sound, and scenery cues for the crew.

"Never go in the wings."

When the Assistant Stage Manager calls "Places," the actors who are in Act I, scene 1, come to the **wings** to be ready for their entrances. There are other people who are in the wings. There is the **Stage Manager** who is "calling" the show, one cue after another, for the sound person and the master electrician and the follow-spot operator. There are also carpenters getting ready to change the scenery between the scenes.

There are dressers in the wings because sometimes actors need to change clothes quickly, and the dressers help them take their clothes on and off. Maria giggles at the thought of Annie or Dracula standing in their underwear in the wings, but Matt says, "Don't be immature." He is very mature.

Of course, there is the Assistant Stage Manager—who does everything for everyone, and still always has time for kids.

Maria wants to be an Assistant Stage Manager when she grows up. And Peter Pan. And the person who hands out the flowers during the curtain call. And a princess!

Sometimes in the wings there are other people—like directors from New York who come to "clean up" the show when it has been out on the road for a long time. Directors become very unhappy when actors don't play their roles the same way at every performance.

The stage door guard—who lets people in to see their friends and accepts flowers from admirers—is not ever supposed to leave the stage door, but sometimes . . .

The investors are very rich. They are called "angels" because they give money to the producer to make the play happen. They are supposed to be in their seats, but sometimes . . .

Everyone likes to be in the wings—it's the closest you can get to the play without actually being in the play. The wings are the borderland between acting and reality. Ordinary actors wait in the wings before they step out and become someone else.

And people in the house will clap their hands . . . and believe.

Matt and Maria like to be in the wings during the **take-in**. Of course, they would like to be in the wings during the show itself, but they are theatre kids, and they know better. Matt and Maria even like to be in the wings when the ghost light is shining on the quiet scenery and they can see Neverland in their minds.

The ghosts join them in the wings.

Take-In
The Take-In is the process of moving all the sets into the theatre for the first time, and hanging the lights and putting the props where they are needed. It is also called the load-in.

"Never go on the fly floor."

Matt and Maria never ever go on the **fly floor**. The Colonial is a hemp house, which means there are many ropes and weights used to lift scenery from the stage level until it is hidden by the curtain tops. Most of the scenery is flown up and out of sight rather than going down into traps under the stage floor.

Backdrops show sunsets or city skylines or mountains. Cars, cabarets, carousels, and Chicago jail cells are flown in and out.

My Fair Lady's scenery includes a flower market, a racetrack, a ballroom, and a library.

The Sound of Music has a mountain, a church, a puppet stage, and a concert hall.

Macbeth—(Whoops! Don't mention *Macbeth* in the theatre. That's bad luck. Call it, "The Scottish Play")—"The Scottish Play" has a castle, a witch's cauldron, and a moving forest.

Peter Pan has Neverland!

"Never go on the stage."

Matt and Maria go on the stage. It is forty-five feet deep and it will hold sixty tons of scenery. They sit in the nursery chairs on the Peter Pan set, confident that they will not break them, but they do not move them from their marks. Matt and Maria go to the **apron** of the stage and pretend to be actors.

Fly Floor
The fly floor or fly gallery is a narrow platform high above one or both sides of the stage where the stagehands stand to pull the ropes to raise and lower the scenery.

Apron
The apron is the part of the stage which is in front of the proscenium arch. What's that? The **proscenium arch** is the large picture-frame opening in the wall through which the audience sees the stage. It often has a huge, heavy curtain which can be raised when the actors are ready to begin the play.

Matt sings, "Don't Cry for Me, Argentina," from *Evita*. He learned it when he was four years old and he's been singing it ever since.

Upstage, Maria climbs onto the *Peter Pan* set. She sings, "It's a Hard-Knock Life," from *Annie*. When she finishes, she starts to sing "A Very Nice Prince," from *Into the Woods*, but Matt says, "One is enough." He knows that she would also like to sing, "There's No Business like Show Business" from *Annie Get Your Gun*. She even likes a song from a musical about Texas (one of those Matt and Maria were not allowed to see). The song is called "Hard Candy Christmas."

Little sisters need to be controlled.

"Race you to the balcony!"

It always works. Maria is off the stage, out the pass door, up the aisle. She reaches the mezzanine, all out of breath. It will take her two or three minutes of yelling, "I beat you, I beat you," to realize that, although it may look like the theatre has a first balcony and a second balcony, it really has a mezzanine and a balcony, and Matt is waiting for her upstairs . . . sitting right on the balcony rail.

Maria says, "You're not supposed to do that— it's really high and dangerous!"

She doesn't know that he waited for her to arrive before he got into that position. It makes him feel just a little queasy, but he would never tell her that.

Matt would not like to play John in *Peter Pan*. Too much flying! He is already way too old to play Michael. He does not mention this to Maria. Little sisters don't need to know everything. Besides, just mention Peter Pan and she will sing all the songs.

Instead, he squeezes his nose between his fingers to make a frosty voice and quotes from Mrs. Philomena: "All the seats face the stage."

The sparkling lights of the chandelier go on. They are very beautiful, especially from the balcony. They are so close the children can almost touch them. This means that the ticket takers, including the very fierce (but nice) ushers, are arriving for the matinee. Their father is checking whether there are enough playbills for everyone in the audience. Wonderful! The theatre is never more exciting than when it is waiting for a show to begin.

Now Matt and Maria know the lights are coming on outside on the marquee, inside in both lobbies, in the orchestra, the mezzanine, the balcony, the ladies' lounge, and even in the gentlemen's room, where nothing much happens, except the usual.

The concessionaire is lining up glasses. He checks the carbonation hose. In the outer lobby, souvenir programs and T-shirts are being displayed. In the inner lobby . . . Junior Mints.

The House Crew is arriving. They are the Colonial stagehands, rather than the ones who travel with each show. They will **strike** the ghost light. Carpenters will move the scenery into position for Act I. There is a nursery with three beds. There is one window upstage. There is a chest of drawers to hide Peter Pan's shadow.

Property people will set the props. There is a stuffed dog and an umbrella. There are leaves under the window. Offstage, there is a poison cake. And there is a Never Bird.

The Electrician will go to "**preset**." Night lights and the Tinker Bell light are ready.

The Sound Technicians will check all the batteries in all the microphones—for Wendy, Smee, Bill Jukes, Tootles, Slightly. The musicians are tuning up in the orchestra pit.

The wardrobe workers will bring clean and pressed costumes to the dressing rooms—an evening gown for Mrs. Darling, a fishtail for the mermaid—and hang clothes in the wings for quick changes. Mr. Darling is also Captain Hook. Matt says, "That tells you something about daddies."

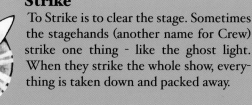

Strike
To Strike is to clear the stage. Sometimes the stagehands (another name for Crew) strike one thing - like the ghost light. When they strike the whole show, everything is taken down and packed away.

Preset
To preset is to place props and costumes and scenery in position before the curtain goes up on a new scene.

The stage door guard will stop doing crossword puzzles. The road crew will arrive. They have traveled with *Peter Pan* to theatres all over the country. The cast comes in off the street in laughing groups of two or three. They don't look much different from Emerson College students, especially the young dancers. Maria wants to go to Emerson College when she grows up.

The Stage Manager will check last night's notes. The Assistant Stage Manager will do everything for everyone.

This afternoon Matt and Maria will get to see what happens after the intermission—again. Matt is rooting for the crocodile.

Of course, they will see the first half all over again. They like to see the shows in the Colonial Theatre over and over again. They are theatre kids.

It's time to go get their tickets.

Thanks

I'm grateful to my husband Donald for this idea, and our son Matthew and daughter Maria, whose exploits in the Colonial Theatre form the core of the story.

Thanks also to the dedicated staffs present and past at the Colonial, Wilbur, Citi-Wang, Shubert, Cutler-Majestic and the Opera House. Some of the names used in this book are meant to honor a dedicated generation of people who worked at the Colonial and Boston's other historic theatres in the early seventies. Thanks for the research provided by Tobie S. Stein's *Boston's Colonial Theatre*, and Jon Platt, publisher.

Brava to Rebecca Rule for her advice, and Jeremy Townsend for her publishing gifts and love of children's books, to Kat Mack for her design skills, and especially to Brandie Kramer whose beautiful illustrations brought this story to life.

About the Author

Maren C. Tirabassi is a best selling author of thirteen books and the former Poet Laureate of Portsmouth, NH. She presents programs for the New Hampshire Humanities Council, leads writing workshops for children and adults and is the pastor of Union Congregational Church, UCC in Madbury, NH. In earlier days, she was a company manager for the legendary Broadway choreographer Agnes de Mille for the Royal Shakespeare Company.

About the Illustrator

Brandie Kramer, a recent graduate of Montserrat College of Art with a Bachelor of Fine Arts degree, works in acrylics, water soluble oils, and pen and ink in a mixed media format. At Montserrat, she directed and designed fashion shows. Her costumes have been seen in productions of Gamaliel Theatre Company. Currently an assistant interior designer in the Concord, NH, area, she is expanding her primary vocation as an illustrator.

The Real
Matt and Maria

The real Matt and Maria are adults now.
Matthew Tirabassi lives in Portsmouth, NH,
and Maria Tirabassi lives in Los Angeles, CA.
Grown up Matt collects big cars and trucks;
grown up Maria did graduate from Emerson
College. They still love to go to shows at the
Colonial Theatre.